BRITANNICA
DISCOVERY
LIBRARY

THE WORLD AROUND US

In this book, you will:

discover interesting things about the world around you.

learn new words.

answer fun questions.

find lots of activities to learn about
the world at the back of the book.

ENCYCLOPÆDIA
Britannica®
GRAND ISLAND PUBLIC LIBRARY

CHICAGO   LONDON   NEW DELHI   PARIS   SEOUL   SYDNEY   TAIPEI   TOKYO

The world around us
is a wonderful place
to play in and explore.

There is so much to learn
about the whole wide world,
and it's waiting just outside your door.

Come on, let's take a look!

Most people live in places that are warm and sunny for much of the year. The other part of the year is colder.

Others live in places where it is hot all the time.

Some people live in parts of the world that never get warm!

What is the world like where you live?

You might live in a big city or a small village.

Maybe you live in the mountains or near a river or an ocean.

What do you see when you go outside?

Imagine living in a different place. What would that place be like?

Wherever you live, it is somewhere on Earth.
We all live together on Earth.

We share the Earth with all kinds of other living things too. But what is the Earth like?

What are some other living things on Earth?

7

The Earth is round. It is made up of land and water.

From space, the Earth looks mostly blue. This is because there is so much water on Earth. Plants, fish, and other animals live in these waters.

Oceans and seas cover most of the land on Earth.
But some of the land rises above the water.

The land above water is where all people live.
Many different plants and animals live on this land too

People, plants, and animals live almost everywhere on Earth.

From space, much of the land on Earth looks green. Other parts look brown. Do you know what makes the land look green? Do you know what the brown parts are?

Trees and other plants give the land its green color. The brown is **desert** land, or other places where few plants grow.

Look at the picture of Earth again. Where are trees growing? Where are places with few plants? Where can you see water?

13

The Earth is made mostly of water and land.
But there is another important part of the
world around us. You can't see it or touch it,
but it is everywhere.

Can you guess what it is?

Here is a hint:

Without it, you couldn't blow bubbles
or blow up a balloon.

15

Without it, birds and planes couldn't fly.
There would be no such thing as kites.
Plants and animals could not stay alive. What is it?

t's air!

ir is all around us. We can't see it or touch it.
ut we all need air to breathe.

Air is always moving around the Earth

The air may be hot or cold, wet or dry. Sometimes the air blows in a gentle breeze.

Other times it becomes a wild wind.

As the air moves, clouds form. Clouds are made of **droplets** of water or bits of ice that stick together in the air above Earth.

Things in the world around us

Clouds hide the sun and then the sun comes out again. Day changes into night.

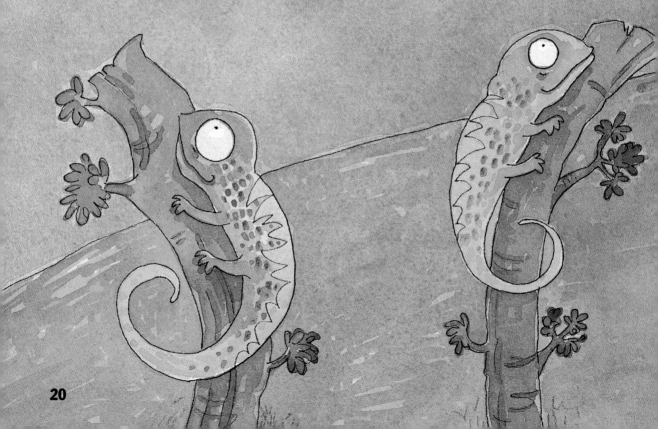

are always changing.

We see different stars in the
ky as the night goes by.

What are
other things
in the world
that change?

The weather is always changing too

Weather can change quickly. When you wake up in the
morning, the sun may be shining bright outside.
The air is warm.

Later, clouds may begin to fill the sky, like big, dark pillows. The air cools off. The wind comes up.

What do you think is going to happen?

The wind rushes through the trees.

Far off, you might hear thunder.
Heavy drops of water splash against the windowpanes.

RAINSTORM!

Inside your house, you may be warm and cozy.
But if you are outside, watch out! You might get wet!

What do you like to do on a rainy day?

Sometimes the rain falls gently.
It might rain for only a few minutes.

Sometimes it rains for days and days.

Rain is good for the Earth.
It gives us water to drink
and helps grow many of the foods we eat.

The trees and grass and flowers
need rain to grow too.

Sometimes rain changes to snow.
When the snow piles up, you might go ice-skating,
have a snowball fight, or build a snowman.

What would
you like to do
in the snow?

The weather changes every day. It may change in only a few hours. The seasons change too. But the seasons change much more slowly.

Think of your last birthday. From that time until your next birthday, four seasons will go by.

The four seasons are winter, spring, summer, and fall, or autumn.

In much of the world, it is easy to tell when the seasons change. In other places, the changes in season are not as easy to see.

Everywhere in the world, winter

By wintertime in some places, many trees have lost their leaves. Their branches are bare like bony arms in the cold.

Sometimes snow falls. You might see your breath if you go outside. You might catch a snowflake on your tongue!

B-r-r-r-r-rrr! It's WINTER!

s the coldest season of the year.

What is winter like where you live?

33

After winter comes spring.

Snow stops falling, but it might rain a lot.
Birds come home after a winter away. The grass and
other plants turn bright green. Lots of colorful flowers
grow. Tiny buds appear on the trees.

Everything is coming back to life!

It's SPRING!

How can you tell when spring has come where you live?

Leaves and grass turn darker green.
Fields of corn and **wheat** grow tall under
the hot summer sun.

of year is summer.

Summer is a good time for trips
to the beach or the pool.
A summer day may be so hot
that you don't feel like doing anything at all!

That's SUMMER!

What do you
like to do in
the summer?

The weather grows cooler

The leaves die and fall from many trees and other plants. Some **crops** of food that have grown through the summer are ready to eat. Farmers bring these crops in from the fields

What do you like best about the fall?

This is the season

again when fall comes.

Many animals gather food to eat
through the long winter too.

called FALL!

What season
do you think
will come next?

Some plants grow in **soil**. Others grow in water.
Some plants even grow on trees.

Plants that grow indoors may look very different from outdoor plants. But all plants are alike in some ways.

Almost every plant has leaves, roots, and seeds. Many have flowers too.

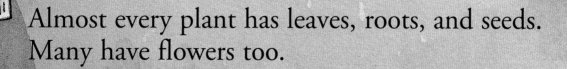

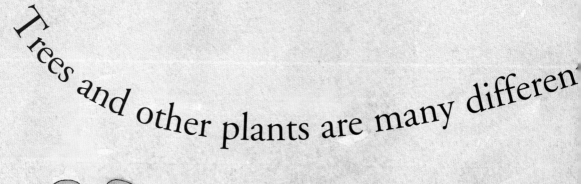

Green plants help make the air we breathe. Thes plants get energy when the Sun shines on their leaves. This gives them the food they need to make more air.

42

hapes and sizes. But most plants are green.

Without green plants, we would have nothing to eat.
We would not even be able to breathe.

Roots are an important

Most plant roots grow in the ground.
The roots help the plants get food from the soil.

Roots that grow
underground often
look like this.

part of plants.

Even plants that grow in water have roots, like these.

Flowers are important too

All flowers have seeds. These seeds give us new plants.

Some seeds fall from the flowers straight to the ground.
Others are carried by the wind and land somewhere else.
These seeds take root in the ground. Then new plants gro

Flowers are important for
another reason.
Some flowers grow into
fruits and vegetables.

What is
your favorite
vegetable?

What is your
favorite fruit?

Look carefully at the fruits and vegetables on the next page. Can you match each one with the tree or the plant below that it comes from?

The Earth is home for all

Everything in our

Plants need sun and rain to grow. People and
animals need plants for the food and air they give us.

living things.

living world is connected.

The changes in the world around us
bring new life and keep us alive.

We must take good care of our

CLEAN AIR

EARTH SHINE

MOON LIGHT

GRE

52

beautiful planet Earth

and everything in it!

THE WORLD AROUND US

GLOSSARY

crops (krops) plants grown usually for food, such as cereals and corn

desert (DEZ ert) a hot, dry, and usually sandy area with little water and where few plants or trees grow

droplets (DROP litz) tiny drops

soil (soyl) the ground or earth in which plants grow

wheat (hweet) a crop that can be made into cereal or ground into flour, which is used in baking breads and cakes

Fun Ways to Learn about THE WORLD AROUND US

Nature's Paintbrushes

1 Take a walk in nature with a friend. Collect two or three fallen tree branches of different kinds and sizes. Look for leafless branches. You might want to collect a pine branch with lots of needles still on it too, if you can find one. When you get home, get out your paints!

Ask a grown-up to hammer the thickest end of the branch until it is flat. This will cause the ends to fan out like a small paintbrush. Use your paintbrush branches to create a colorful painting! For the pine branches, just dip the needles directly into the paint.

What other things can you think of to paint with?

Sparkly Snowflakes

2 Even if there is no snow where you live, you can have snowflakes! Ask a grown-up for several white paper coffee filters. (Use plain white paper cut in large circles if you don't have coffee filters.) Flatten the filters as much as possible. Using watercolors or watered-down tempera paints, paint the coffee filters in snowflake colors—gray, pale blue, dark blue, silver.

Meanwhile, have a grown-up help you add lots of salt to a cup of hot water. Stir to mix it together and let the water cool. Now dip your brush in the saltwater and paint a thin layer of it over the paper filters.

When they are dry, fold each paper filter in half. Then fold each one in half again. Finally, fold in half one last time.

Cut into the folded sides and the edges to make patterns. Be careful to leave some of the folded edges uncut. Now unfold your snowflakes. The dried saltwater should make them sparkle!

Adopt a Plant!

3 How good are you at noticing changes in the living world around you? Here is a fun way to see changes you might not have noticed before. To start, pick a plant somewhere near your house. You will be watching what happens to it over time. For instance, adopt a small, young tree whose leaves you can see up close, or choose a tomato plant, a rosebush, or other growing thing. Visit your adopted plant every few days and see if you see anything different about it. Does it have new flowers? Is it losing leaves? Are more insects crawling in it than last time you checked?

Use a small notebook or make your own by stapling blank pages between a construction-paper cover. Put the date at the top of the page every time you write down something new about your adopted plant. You could include drawings of the changes. You might even add photographs. How does your plant look different as the season passes? If you watch your plant for a whole year, you will probably see a lot of changes!

"Play is a child's work." It is through play that children learn, as they are often much more receptive when the activities are fun, engaging, and things they have chosen to do. Being outside provides them different opportunities to sharpen their senses by seeing, touching, smelling, and hearing, all while moving around freely. Here are some ways to enhance the activities on the previous page.

Nature's Paintbrushes. Small branches and twigs can be dipped in paint to be used almost like pencils. But by flattening the end of the branch, the fibrous insides will be exposed, making a great little paintbrush. If your child has collected long branches, cut them down so that they are very short and easy to use. A bit more messy but a lot of fun for children is to dip other plant parts in paint too. They could paint using the bushy stem of a plant, a small fern, or a palm frond, for instance. Older children might enjoy arranging different shaped leaves on a piece of paper and then painting over them. After your child has painted over the leaves and the paper is dry, carefully remove the leaves. The leaf silhouettes make a great piece of children's art!

Sparkly Snowflakes. Younger children may need a bit of help folding and cutting the snowflake patterns for this activity. If they want to cut their own shapes, however, let them do so, even if the shapes don't end up perfect. To get the most sparkly effect, make sure the hot water is heavily saturated with salt. Experiment to see how much salt you will need per cup of water. For younger children, either cut some snowflake shapes for them or just let them paint on plain paper and then add a saltwater layer last. Hang the snowflakes with thread or craft wire or just tape them to your windows.

Adopt a Plant! This activity is a great way to help children increase their powers of observation and learn about the cycles of plant life at the same time. Take a walk with your child, even if just around the yard, down the street, or to a nearby park, and explain the object of the activity. If possible, guide him or her to plants that might go through more rapid changes so that the changes will be apparent more quickly, but don't insist. The younger your child is the more you'll want to pick a plant that will go through changes quickly—or perhaps do this activity during a time of year when there are obvious changes in the foliage around you.

Illustrations by Johanna Boccardo.

Page 48: Photos: Corbis; (top right) Bernardo Bucci; (bottom left) Bradley Smith. Page 49: Photos: Corbis; (top left) Ed Bohon; (top right) Bernardo Bucci; (bottom left) Owaki—Kulla; (bottom right) Lew Robertson.

© 2005, 2008 by Encyclopædia Britannica, Inc.

International Standard Book Number: 978-1-59339-426-4

Britannica Discovery Library:
Volume 4: The World Around Us 2005, 2008

Britannica.com may be accessed on the Internet at http://www.britannica.com.

Encyclopædia Britannica, Britannica, and the Thistle logo are registered trademarks of Encyclopædia Britannica, Inc.